40690
Pinkie Flamingo

Dave/David Sargent
AR B.L.: 4.6
Points: 0.5   LG

Pinkie Flamingo

David M. Sargent, Jr., and his friends live in Northwest Arkansas. His writing career began in 1995 with a cruel joke being played on his mother. The friends pictured with him are (from left to right) Vera, Buffy, and Mary.

Dave Sargent is a lifelong resident of the small town of Prairie Grove, Arkansas. A fourth-generation dairy farmer, Dave began writing in early December 1990. He enjoys the outdoors and has a real love for birds and animals.

Pinkie Flamingo

By

Dave Sargent
and
David M. Sargent, Jr.

Beyond The End
By
Sue Rogers

Illustrated by
Jane Lenoir

Ozark Publishing, Inc.
P.O. Box 228
Prairie Grove, AR 72753

Cataloging-in-publication data

Sargent, Dave, 1941-
　Pinkie Flamingo / by Dave Sargent ; illustrated by
Jane Lenoir. – Prairie Grove, AR : Ozark Publishing,
c2003.
　　vi, 42 p. : col. ill. ; 21 cm.　(Feather tale series)

　"Leaving home"—Cover.
　SUMMARY: Pinkie the flamingo teaches young
Brutus the bear the importance of having respect for
the property of others. Includes factual information on
flamingos.
　ISBN: 1-56763-747-7　(hc)
　　　　1-56763-748-5　(pbk)
　RL 2.4 ; IL 2-8

　[1. Flamingos—Fiction.　2. Bears—Fiction.] I.
Lenoir, Jane, 1950- ill. II. Title. III. Series.

　PZ10.3.S243Pi 2003
　[Fic]—dc21　　　　　　　　　　　　99-087655

Inspired by

my many drives through Louisiana where, if I'm lucky, I catch a glimpse of the beautiful pink-colored flamingo.

Dedicated to

all students who enjoy looking at flamingo pictures.

Foreword

Pinkie Flamingo teaches young Brutus the Bear the importance of having respect for others' property. Of course, Pinkie gets a little help from Farmer John's rock-salt shotgun.

Contents

One   Tired of Mama's Rules   1

Two   Juicy Red Strawberries 13

Three   Brutus Makes Amends 23

Four   Flamingo Facts   31

If you would like to have an author of The Feather Tale Series visit your school, free of charge, call 1-800-321-5671 or 1-800-960-3876.

One

Tired of Mama's Rules

Sunlight danced on the dew of the tall reeds in the big zoo in the state of Louisiana. Pinkie Flamingo sighed a big sigh and closed her eyes. "My tummy is full," she thought, "and the zoo is closed for the day, so I may as well take a nap." Her pink feathers glistened beneath the sun's rays as she tucked one long skinny leg beneath her belly. Seconds later, her eyes flew open again.

"Just one problem," the big bird mumbled. "I'm not sleepy!"

Using long slow strides, Pinkie walked around the enclosure that contained grass, a big pond, and huge rocks.

"I have a really nice home," she scolded herself. "Why is it that I am so restless today?"

Suddenly she made a discovery. The zookeeper had accidentally left the gate unlatched. She cocked her head to one side and welcomed the invitation to travel. Hmmm . . .

"Yes!" Pinkie decided happily. "I'll just visit the countryside and return within an hour or two."

Thirty minutes later, she was soaring above the trees with her long neck and legs extended, creating streamlined high flight. She honked greetings to ducks and geese as she traveled over the hills of Arkansas.

Suddenly loud noises on the ground below caught her attention, and she slowly circled the trouble spot. A small black furry critter was

whining and slapping at the air with
both paws.

"Oh my," she said. "I better see if I can help that poor little fellow. He seems to be in serious trouble."

She gracefully landed a short distance from the upset youngster. Honey was dripping from his mouth, and angry bees were attacking from every direction.

"Run!" Pinkie Flamingo yelled. "Run to the pond and jump in."

Without a moment's hesitation, the furry little animal scampered through the maze of flying insects and made a dive that landed him right in the deep cool water.

Pinkie Flamingo waited a short time before walking to the edge of the pond to check on the little black bear. His nose was the only part of his body that was exposed, and Pinkie smiled as he began to fight his way back to the bank of the pond.

"What's so funny?" he growled as he sloshed toward Pinkie.

Hiding a smile, Pinkie replied, "Nothing. Are you okay?"

"Of course I'm okay," he said in a husky voice. "My mama thinks I'm still a baby. She says I'm not old enough yet to go out hunting alone. Well, I'm tired of her silly old rules! I can take care of myself!" the little black bear growled. "And that's just what I'm gonna do!"

"What is your name?" Pinkie asked.

"My name is Brutus. I am the most ferocious bear in these woods," he said smugly.

Pinkie laughed, which sparked a tantrum from the angry little bear. He began stomping his hind paw. Then, he fell to his knees and pounded the dirt with his front paws. He growled, snarled, and snapped as though fighting a ferocious enemy.

The bird waited patiently until the bear was too tired to continue. Panting, wheezing, and completely out of ornery ideas, the irate little bear rolled over on his back.

"Well now, do you feel better?" Pinkie Flamingo asked.

The little bear just glared at her without speaking.

"If you are going to be Brutus, the most ferocious bear in the woods," the flamingo said quietly, "you need to learn the rules of the big world."

Young Brutus Bear stood up and shook his head.

"I left home," Brutus growled, "because I was tired of rules. It's just not fair! Big bears don't have rules!"

Well, Pinkie instantly flew mad! She folded her wings behind her and paced back and forth in front of the little bear. Briefly, she paused to glare at Brutus and mutter to herself.

When Pinkie Flamingo regained her composure, she cleared her throat to speak.

"Young man, everyone has rules to follow! Little, big, or in between does not matter. Everybody," Pinkie repeated, "lives a better life because of rules!"

"Do not!" he shouted.

"Do too!" she squealed.

A faint "do not" was lost amid the flapping of wings as an irritated Pinkie prepared to leave the problem cub.

"Why don't you stick around a while?" little Brutus Bear yelled as Pinkie lifted off the ground. "Wait! I'm going to Farmer John's berry patch now. Farmer John has one big strawberry patch just waitin' to be eaten. Want some?"

Pinkie groaned, but she decided against offering more advice. She watched Brutus the mischievous bear scamper toward the clearing.

Two

Juicy Red Strawberries

The flamingo knew she had made a mistake when she decided to circle over the farm. "I can't go now," she thought. "That little bear is about to get in bad trouble." After extending long legs and neck to the max, she frantically flapped her wings for greater speed.

Brutus ran around a tall stack of crates and was entering a great big strawberry patch as Pinkie glided downward. By the time she landed, the little bear was stuffing a paw full

of red strawberries into his mouth
and reaching for more.

"You are not yet ready to leave your mama," Pinkie said hoarsely. "You are too undisciplined!"

Brutus flashed her a juicy red smile before grabbing another handful of strawberries. Pinkie noticed damaged leaves, vines, and wasted fruit littering the ground around him as he slurped, burped, and chomped.

Suddenly, without any warning, a loud 'BOOM' shattered the stillness of the morning.

"Molly," Farmer John yelled, "come quick! Look what I see in your strawberry patch. Unless I get rid of this rascal right now, you won't have anything left."

Pinkie stared in horror as the man ran across the barnyard toward them. His face was flushed in anger as he aimed his shotgun at Brutus.

"Run, Brutus!" she screamed.

The terrified little bear began to race blindly through the strawberry patch. Seconds later, he ran into the garden and trampled tomatoes, bell peppers, okra, green beans, and stalks of corn beneath his paws. There was even more damage done as he ran searching for a safe haven.

Suddenly a woman's frantic scream sent Pinkie airborne.

"My beautiful strawberry crop was due to be packed up and shipped out tomorrow," she cried. "And that mean little bear has destroyed it!"

Another 'BOOM' echoed amid the farm buildings, and Pinkie dived low for a better look at little Brutus' ongoing bad luck. She must do something to help him.

"John! Look at that!" Molly yelled. "It's a pink flamingo!"

"Dadburnit, Molly! Flamingos don't live in Arkansas," Farmer John growled. "I'm after that pesky bear!"

"John, the flamingo is landing!" Molly squealed. "Don't scare her."

Farmer John lowered the gun and looked where she was pointing.

"You're right, Molly," he said. "The zoo needs to know about her."

"Let's go talk to them, John. I'll pick and pack what strawberries are left when we get back."

Pinkie breathed a sigh of relief as she saw Brutus the Bear disappear into the blackberry thicket in back of the big hay barn. Moments later, she watched Farmer John and Molly climb in their truck and drive away.

"Pssst, Brutus," she whispered. "Where are you? We need to talk!"

After listening for a response and hearing none, she walked into the woods and called once again. This time she heard a strange sound. Peering around a large tree trunk, she saw young Brutus sitting on a log. His small body was shaking, and tears were streaming down his face.

"Aw, poor little fellow," she murmured softly. "Everything is all right now. Don't cry."

The little bear softly hiccupped and coughed before yet another sob shook his furry body.

"I know how we can correct your mistakes," Pinkie said, "so will you please stop crying?"

Young Brutus hiccupped, wiped away his tears, and nodded.

"Good!" Pinkie said. "Now this is the plan. You will begin by . . ."

Three

Brutus Makes Amends

A short time later, both Pinkie and Brutus were hurrying through the woods and out into the clearing. Within minutes, they were standing in the strawberry patch.

"Okay, Brutus," Pinkie said in a hushed voice. "Do your thing!"

Brutus grinned and nodded.

"Sure will, Ms. Pinkie," he said. "And I'll do it in record time."

"I'm sure you will," she said with a smile.

Pinkie felt pride rise within her

as the little bear quickly began filling
the crates with the ripened fruit.

Three hours later, Pinkie awoke from a nap to find little Brutus curled up beside her.

"Oh no!" she groaned. "I must have fallen asleep. I should have kept my eyes on this little critter."

The little bear snored gently as Pinkie stood up and walked over to the strawberry patch.

"Well for goodness sake!" she gasped as her gaze stopped on the neatly picked and packed crates of strawberries. Bright sunlight danced upon the plump red fruit as though boasting of a bountiful harvest. She hurried over to the sleeping bear cub and patted him gently on the head with one wing.

"Now, young man, you are truly a fine black bear of these woods," she murmured softly. "Your mama is going to be very proud of you."

Suddenly the sound of a vehicle broke the stillness of the afternoon. The flamingo gasped as she watched Farmer John and Molly get out of their truck. Then the feathers stood straight up on her head when they headed toward the garden.

"Pssst, wake up, young Brutus," Pinkie whispered. "Please wake up. Farmer John and Molly are home!"

The tired little bear immediately leaped to his feet, wide-eyed and scared skinny.

"Run to the woods," she yelled. "Hurry!"

Young Brutus Bear scampered from the strawberry patch and raced toward the nearby woods. In hopes of drawing attention away from the little bear, Pinkie frantically flapped her wings and honked. But only moments later, she realized that her plan was in vain.

"That dadburned little ole black bear is back! Reckon he's after those strawberries again!" Farmer John yelled. "I'm gonna get my rock-salt shotgun and let him have it!"

As the man raced back to the house, Molly ran toward the garden.

"Uh-oh!" Pinkie gasped. "I'm out of here!" And within seconds, the pink bird was circling high above the rows of neatly packed crates.

Molly ran into the strawberry patch and screeched to a halt. Her eyes widened in wonder as she looked at each neatly picked and packed crate of strawberries.

"How much damage did he do this time?" Farmer John shouted as he ran toward her with his shotgun tightly clutched in one hand.

"No damage, John," Molly said in a loud voice. "Look at this. I think that little fellow is a friend of ours!"

Pinkie smiled as she watched Farmer John and Molly admire young Brutus' accomplishments. She sighed before taking flight toward the nearby woods. Pride soared within her as she looked down and saw Brutus hugging his mama. He waved as she glided low over their heads.

Pinkie Flamingo gained altitude and veered to the left, turning toward her home in the zoo.

"I think," she said, "that young Brutus, ferocious bear of the woods, will now be known as young Brutus, the wisest bear in the woods. Oh no! I left the zoo without permission! Perhaps that little bear critter is more sensible than me!" Hmmm . . .

Four

Flamingo Facts

A common name for the five species of a family of birds having exceptionally long legs and long flexible necks is *flamingo*. Their relationship to other birds is a bit uncertain. Some evidence puts them with the herons and ibises, some with geese and ducks, and there is fossil evidence that suggests a slight relationship to shorebirds. About midway, the bill bends downward. The upper mandible is very narrow and fits into the lower like the lid of a box. When flamingos feed, they dip their head under water and scoop backward with it upside down.

The edges of a flamingo's bill have tiny narrow transverse plates called lamellae. The big fleshy tongue presses against the inside of the bill and strains the water out through the lamellae, leaving behind small invertebrates and vegetable matter, which the bird eats.

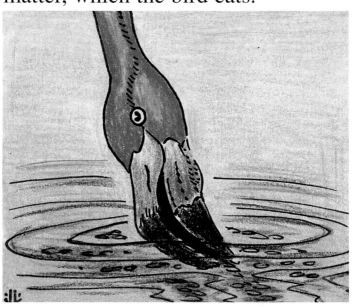

The largest species of flamingos is the greater flamingo. It has two subspecies: one is a vivid red, and the other is paler. The first of these breeds is found in the Caribbean area, from Yucatán and the West Indies to the coast of northeastern South America. It also breeds well in captivity, and sometimes a flamingo is seen north of Florida. (Some believe it escaped from a zoo.) The paler flamingo can be found in Eurasia, the Mediterranean area and Africa, east to India. Males of both of these subspecies may reach sixty-one inches (over 5 feet) in height.

The greater flamingo usually breeds in standing water or on low islands in shallow ponds, lagoons, and salt pans. It builds a conical mound of mud and makes a slight depression in the top of it. It lays one egg. Occasionally it lays two eggs.

The young can feed themselves after thirty days, but they will eat

regurgitated food from a parent for as long as seventy-five days.

The Chilean flamingo is a little smaller than the greater flamingo. It is pale pink with bright red streaks on the back. It builds its nest in high salt lakes in the Andes and also in the

ANDEAN FLAMINGO

JAMES'S FLAMINGO

LESSER FLAMINGO

lowlands of southern South America.

The Andean and the James's, or Puna, also live in the Andes. These are small. The lesser flamingo of Africa east to India is the smallest of all the species. The lesser flamingo has a world population of 4 million.

Scientific classification: Flamingos make up the *Phoenicopteridae* family of the order *Ciconiiformes*. They are sometimes placed in their own order, *Phoenicopteriformes*. The greater flamingo is classified as *Phoenicopterus ruber*, its vivid red subspecies as *Phoenicopterus ruber ruber*, and its paler subspecies as *Phoenicopterus ruber roseus*. The Chilean flamingo is classified as *Phoenicopterus chilensis*, the Andean flamingo as *Phoenicopterus andinus*, James's flamingo as *Phoenicopterus jamesi*, and the lesser flamingo as *Phoenicopterus minor*.

BEYOND "THE END" . . .

LANGUAGE LINKS

Pinkie explained to Brutus that "...everyone has rules to follow. Little, big, or in between does not matter. Everybody." Of course, Brutus argued. Who was right?

Make a time line beginning when you were two years old and go to age twenty-two. In each year, list the rules you were taught to go by—rules at home, at school, when you are shopping, visiting, etc. Think about what rules will apply when you begin to drive, to move away from home, to work and make money, to vote, etc. Will all rules disappear after you are twenty-two?

CURRICULUM CONNECTIONS

On her unexpected flight leaving the zoo, Pinkie honked greetings to ducks and geese as she traveled over the hills of Arkansas. Which of these states does not border Arkansas?
Texas
Louisiana
Mississippi
Kansas
Missouri

A boy studied his spelling words for 22 minutes. He studied his math flashcards for 16 minutes. He watched TV for 65 minutes. How long did he study?

THE ARTS

Hundreds of thousands of plastic pink flamingos are sold for lawn decorations, wedding decorations, and house-warming gifts every year. Authentic flamingos always have their creator, Don Featherstone's, signature under their tails. Each has a yellow beak with a black tip. They are only sold in pairs.

Make a giant flamingo for your classroom wall. Print the drawing of a flamingo you can find at web site <www.enchantedlearning.com/subjects/birds/printouts/Flamingo amer.shtml>. Use an opaque projector to enlarge the flamingo drawing to any size you want. Trace the outline onto a large strip of bulletin board paper. Before moving the pro-jector, trace the pink parts of the flamingo, including legs, onto pink bulletin board paper—including details; trace the beak and eyes on orange paper; and the tip of the beak on black paper as shown. Go over the details inside each part with a black marker. Cut out pieces and glue to the large outline. Ta-Dah! A masterpiece!

THE BEST I CAN BE

Brutus made a mistake. All of us make mistakes. We show our true character by how we correct our mistakes. Vince Lombardi once said, "The greatest accomplishment is not in never falling, but in rising again after you fall." And Babe Ruth said, "Never let the fear of striking out get in your way." Remember that Mr. Ruth held not only the homerun record but also the strikeout record! I like what Josh Billings said, "Consider the postage stamp: its usefulness consists in the ability to stick to one thing till it gets there." The great mathematician and physicist Albert Einstein once said, "Anyone who has never made a mistake has never tried anything new."

Don't you admire all these people? You will also admire Dave Sargent, who wrote this book with his son David. Dave Sargent had a huge problem—it was impossible for him to learn to read when he was in school. But like the postage stamp, he stuck to his dream and is now a famous writer of over 150 books!

Discuss these sayings by famous people. Think about them when you have made a mistake.